LUCKY LUKAS

LAIMINGAS LUKAS

Story by Jura Reilly
Illustrations by Ted Reilly

Set in Garamond Premier Pro
Typeset by BookPOD

ISBN: 978-0-6482038-4-1 [print]
ISBN: 978-0-6482038-5-8 [E-Book]

A catalogue record for this
book is available from the
NATIONAL
LIBRARY National Library of Australia
OF AUSTRALIA

For our grandchildren

Grace, Oliver, Pearl & Milo

Lucky Lukas / Laimingas Lukas was written to encourage
children to persist in striving to attain their goals, whether
in a sport or in their studies. Like our first book *Laima's
Lunch / Laimos Pietūs*, it is presented in two languages for
families who want their children to learn Lithuanian.

Reading this story with your children will give them
an opportunity to discuss their aspirations and to
explore the situations raised in the back section.

A child's participation in team sports encourages healthy
development and socialisation, bringing a family together
in the endeavours and rewards all sports can bring.

Lukas always wanted to be as tall as his uncle Jonas.
Lukas visada norėjo būti toks aukštas kaip jo dėdė Jonas.

Why? Because Lukas wanted to be the best basketball player at his school.
Kodėl? Todėl kad Lukas norėjo būti geriausias krepšininkas jo mokykloje.

From the time he could first throw a ball, Lukas practised at home every day.

Nuo to laiko, kaip jis išmoko mesti kamuolį, Lukas praktikavosi kasdien namuose.

One day, Lukas heard about a new basketball team at his school.

Vieną dieną Lukas išgirdo apie naują krepšinio komandą jo mokykloje.

He asked his friends if they would like to play with the team.

Jis paklausė draugų, ar jie norėtų žaisti su komanda.

'No! We prefer football.'

‚Ne! Mums patinka futbolas.'

Lukas was determined to try out for the team.

Lukas pasiryžo pabandyti patekti į komandą.

His parents went to S-Mart and bought him a pair of basketball boots.

Jo tėvai nuvažiavo į S-Martą ir nupirko jam krepšinio batus.

Lukas was very nervous at the tryout for the basketball team. He was afraid he would not be selected.

Lukas labai jaudinosi krepšinio komandos bandyme. Jis bijojo, kad nebus išrinktas.

Lukas was happy to have been selected for the team. He was a fast runner, but his team-mates would not pass the ball to him.

Lukas džiaugėsi, kad buvo išrinktas į komandą. Jis buvo greitas bėgikas, tačiau komandos draugai neperdavė jam kamuolio.

Lukas was sad because he sat on the bench for most of the practice matches.
Lukui buvo liūdna, nes per daugumą rungtynių, jis sėdėjo ant atsarginių suolo.

One night after practice at the stadium, Lukas overheard the other boys talking. 'What do you think about that Lukas?'

Vieną naktį po treniruotės stadione, Lukas išgirdo kitus berniukus kalbant. ‚Ką Jus galvojat apie tą Luką?‘

They started to laugh. 'Such a loser! Just have a look at his shoes. Pure S-Mart!'

Jie pradėjo juoktis. ‚Toks nevykėlis! Tiesiog pažvelk į jo batus. Grynas S-Martas!‘

Lukas went red with embarrassment and slowly walked home.

Lukas paraudo su gėda, ir lėtai nuėjo namo.

'Dad, why can't I have real basketball boots, like the other guys?'

‚Tėte, kodėl negaliu turėti tikrus krepšio batus, kaip kiti berniukai?'

His father replied, 'Son, you know how hard your mother and I work. We cannot afford to buy you, or your sisters, expensive things'.

Jo tėvas atsakė: ‚Sūnau, tu žinai, kaip sunkiai mes su mama dirbame. Mes negalime, tau ne tavo seserims nupirkti brangių daiktų'.

Lukas knew there was no use in arguing.

Lukas žinojo kad neapsimoka ginčytis.

'We will all come and watch your first match', his mother promised.

‚Mes visi atvažiuosime ir stebėsime tavo pirmąsias rungtynes', pažadėjo jo mama.

The night of Lukas's first game came. He put on his uniform and laced up his black boots.

Atėjo pirmojo Luko žaidimo naktis. Jis apsivilko uniformą ir suvarstė juodus batus.

The siren went and the game began, but Lukas sat on the bench with his coach.

Sirena suskambėjo ir prasidėjo rungtynės, bet Lukas sėdėjo ant suolo su treneriu.

In the last 5 minutes, Lukas's team was two points behind. Suddenly Erik, their best player, slipped and fell onto the floor.

Per paskutines 5 minutes Luko komanda atsiliko dviem taškais. Staiga geriausias jų žaidėjas Erikas paslydo ir nukrito ant grindų.

'That's the end for Erik', said the coach. 'Lukas, you will have to take his place.'

‚Tai Erikui pabaiga', sakė treneris. ‚Lukai, tu turėsi užimti jo vietą.'

As before, Lukas's team-mates did not pass the ball to him. There were only a few minutes until the final siren.

Kaip ir anksčiau, Luko komandos draugai neperdavė jam kamuolio. Liko tik kelios minutės iki paskutinės sirenos.

Suddenly, while the other team was passing the ball, Lukas managed to intercept it.

Staiga, kai kita komanda perdavė kamuolį, Lukas sugebėjo ji perimti.

Lukas knew that had to try for a 3-pointer. Could he do it?

Lukas žinojo kad jis turi pabandyti tritaškį. Ar jis galėtų tai padaryti?

Lukas took a deep breath. Now was his chance to prove to everyone that he was a good basketballer.

Lukas giliai įkvėpė. Dabar buvo jo galimybė įrodyti visiems, kad jis geras krepšininkas.

Lukas leapt into the air and threw the ball, just like uncle Jonas had taught him.

Lukas šoko į orą ir metė kamuolį taip kaip dėdė Jonas jį pamokė.

The ball spun through the air in a perfect arc and dropped through the net.

Kamuolys puikiu lanku pasisuko per orą ir krito pro tinklą.

Lukas's team had won! The players hoisted Lukas onto their shoulders. He was a hero!
Luko komanda laimėjo! Žaidėjai pakėlė Luką ant pečių! Jis buvo didvyris!

Dad and uncle Jonas each gave Lukas a big high-five, and his mother gave him a gentle hug.
Tėtis ir dėdė Jonas kiekvienas davė Lukui didelį aukštą penketą, o jo mama ji švelniai apkabino.

Suddenly, a man approached the happy family. 'How would you like to join VYTIS, our local Lithuanian basketball team? We need good players like you!'

Staiga prie laimingos šeimos priėjo vyras. 'Ar norėtum prisijungti prie mūsų vietinės Lietuvių krepšinio komandos VYTIS? Mums reikia tokių gerų žaidėjų kaip tu!'

Lukas's father whispered quietly to him, 'See, you don't need brand name basketball shoes to win the game. Victory comes from the heart!'

Luko tėvas tyliai jam sušnibždėjo: ‚Matai, norint laimėti žaidimą nereikia firminių krepšinio batų. Pergalė kyla iš širdies!‘

The next day at school, everyone was still talking about his winning 3-pointer.

Kitą dieną mokykloje visi kalbėjo apie jo laimėtą tritaškį.

From that day on, everyone called him "Lucky Lukas".

Nuo tos dienos visi jį vadino „Laimingas Lukas".

DISCUSSION POINTS

Why did Lukas's team-mates tease him about the boots he was wearing?

How would you feel if you had been Lukas?

What would you have done if you had been Lukas?

Does it matter what sort of basketball gear you wear at school?

Does it matter what sort of basketball gear you wear in a game?

Have any of your friends, or school mates, been mean or rude to you?

Why? What happened?

How can a coach help his team work together?

How important is the captain for your team?

How can you help make your team a better group?

DRILLS & SKILLS

Healthy diet: Eat healthily, limit take-aways, soft drinks and sodas. Refuse cigarettes & illegal drugs. You have only one body: it's irreplaceable!

Keeping fit: Walk or ride a bicycle to school, walk or run at least a mile a day & listen to your coach's advice about specific exercises.

Athletic skills: Basketball requires sudden acceleration, sharp turns, quick stops and constant movement. Learn & practice the techniques. Don't miss any practices unless you are sick.

Ball skills: Learn the skills needed for dribbling, intercepting, passing and shooting goals.

3 on 3: it's now an Olympics sport!

Know the Rules: Once you've been playing for a while, volunteer to referee a game.

Respect the coach, the referees & your team: All are volunteers who passionately love the game.

BASKETBALLERS

Investigate one or more famous basketball players. Find out as much as you can about their youth, first clubs, who has influenced them and their playing styles. Find some video footage of your player. Write up a report and post it to your team's website. You could also prepare a school project. Here are some starters ...

Lithuania

Arvydas Sabonis, Domantas Sabonis, Šarūnas Marčiulionis, Pranas Liubinas, Jonas Valančiunas, Rimas Kurtinaitis, Šarunas Jasikevičius, Elena Kubiliūnaitė-Garbačiauskienė, Eglė Šulčiutė & Gintarė Petronytė.

More info:

https://en.wikipedia.org/wiki/List_of_Lithuanian_NBA_players

https://en.wikipedia.org/wiki/Lithuania_women%27s_national_basketball_team

Australia

Leonas Baltrūnas, Algis Ignatavičius, Ed Palubinskas & Andrew Svaldenis.

RULES

Level 0 (beginners)

https://websites.sportstg.com/get_file.cgi?id=444646

FIBA https://basketballvictoria.com.au/rules-of-the-game/

Interested in refereeing?

https://vbra.basketball.net.au/referee-education/

Women's Basketball

https://en.wikipedia.org/wiki/Women%27s_basketball
[n.b. ball & court dimensions]

Videos

1. The Basic Rules of Basketball:
   https://www.youtube.com/watch?v=XbtmGKif7Ck

2. Better Basketball:
   https://www.youtube.com/watch?v=cv9XOWDp_pA

3. South Korea vs Lithuania 2020
   https://www.youtube.com/watch?v=OK2O8dFTSsg

& there's much more to discover about this sport!

ACKNOWLEDGEMENTS

Anita & David Reilly, for their comments on the text.

Astrid Līberts and Ilze Avitabile, for comments on the illustrations.

Geelong Lithuanian Sports Club, *Vytis*.

Bruno Tarantino at SCS Geelong for technical assistance.

Sylvie Blair and colleagues at BookPod, for preparation of the text and illustrations for publication.

IngramSpark, for production, publication & distribution services.

ABOUT THE AUTHORS

JURA REILLY is an Australian-Lithuanian author of four previous books; *A Wolf At Our Door / Vilkas prie mūsų durų* (2013), *Circle of Amber* (2014) and *Sylvia's Book Smuggler* (2018). These drew upon stories told by her great-aunts, Irena and Viktoria, who had endured many years of exile in Siberia and her immediate family, who had migrated as Displaced Persons to Australia in the wake of WW2. She also published a children's storybook, *Laima's Lunch / Laimos Pietūs* (2020).

Jura's other interests:

Making amber jewellery: *See Amber by Jura*

https://www.facebook.com/Amber-by-Jura-587156698059625

She also administers 2 Facebook groups:

Baltics in Australia:

https://www.facebook.com/groups/balticinaustralia/

Baltica,: which now has over 4000 members: https://www.facebook.com/groups/291014531051707/

Laima's Lunch / Laimos Pietūs can be purchased online worldwide through Amazon etc, as can Circle of Amber and *Sylvia's Book Smuggler.*

Circle Of Amber: https://www.amazon.com/Circle-Amber-Jura-Reilly/dp/0995386803

Sylvia's Book Smuggler: https://www.amazon.com.au/Sylvias-Book-Smuggler-Jura-Reilly/ dp/0648203808

Copies of *A Wolf At Our Door* can be bought on E-Bay or directly from the author at jurareilly@hotmail.com.

TED REILLY is the founding editor of an international literary journal *Azuria* and has published a collection of poetry, *Three Poets,* in conjunction with Robert Drummond & Grant Fraser (2019).

He has a long-standing involvement in Australia's Lithuanian community, dancing with Melbourne's folk group *Klumpakojis* in the 1970s, serving 10 years as secretary of Geelong's Lithuanian community and singing in the choir, *Viltis*. He first visited Lithuania in 1992. In 2003 he taught English as a second language in Druskininkai & Kaunas for two months, publishing a memoir, *First Snow*, based on this experience. He also has had his poetry translated into Lithuanian and has participated in the Spring Poetry Festival. In 2004 he was awarded a Silver Medal of Honour by Lithuania's President Valdas Adamkus for service to the Lithuanian community. Ted has continued his involvement in the Lithuanian community by organising the Literature afternoons as part of the Biannual Australian Lithuanian Culture Festival. Both his children have played basketball for *Vytis* Geelong.

In 2015, Ted resumed a long-standing interest in art, learning to paint in oils, illustrating his poetry chapbooks and successfully showing at local art exhibitions. After being introduced to watercolour, Ted produced a series of cartoons, landscapes and greeting cards. In 2020 he published *Virus*, a chapbook of satirical cartoons. *Laima's Lunch/Laimos Pietūs* and *Lucky Lukas / Laimingas Lukas* are his latest forays into book illustration.

He can be contacted at tedreilly100@hotmail.com.